W9-AJO-780

The Day Abuelo Got Lost

Diane de Anda
illustrated by Alleanna Harris

Albert Whitman & Company
Chicago, Illinois

Abuelo has lived with me, Mama, and Papi all my life.

The four of us have always been la familia.

After school, before my parents got home from work, was Abuelo's and my special time together. We built model planes, cars, and boats on the worktable in the garage.

"This piece goes here, Luis," Abuelo said. Then
he smiled as he watched me glue it in place.

Sometimes, Abuelo spread paper across the worktable, and we painted together. I painted houses and trees, and Abuelo put in all the people.

"Here's your mamá with her long hair and your papá with his hat. Here I am with my mustache, and there you are, Luis, with your big smile," he said.

Sometimes he drew our big brown dog, Sancho.

Afterward, Abuelo made quesadillas for us to snack on. He laughed when I nibbled on the cheese that oozed out all over my fingers.

Then he told me stories about his adventures
with his dog Café when he was a little boy in Mexico.

After a while, Abuelo couldn't remember how the pieces fit together, so we stopped building models. But we still painted, side by side.

Then Mama said we couldn't use the stove anymore, because Abuelo kept forgetting to turn it off. So we made peanut butter and jelly sandwiches together instead.

"Tell me a story about you and Café," I begged.
Abuelo started telling his stories, but would get confused
and stop in the middle.

He'd wrinkle his forehead and think really hard, then look around and pat Sancho on the top of his head and say, "Good boy, Café."

We still painted on the workbench together, but he called me Chico instead of Luis. I wanted to say, "Abuelo, don't you remember my name is Luis?" But I didn't.

One day when I came home, Abuelo was not there.
I looked in the garage, and I called for him all through
the house, but he did not answer.

Mama talked to the neighbors, then stayed home
and waited for him.

Papi and I got in the car and drove up and down streets looking for him.

We found Abuelo standing on a corner a few blocks
away, looking all around.

He looked upset and called Papi señor instead of hijo.

Everything changed the day Abuelo got lost. Now he stays in a different house during the day, with other abuelos and abuelas and people who take care of him so he won't get lost again.

But at the end of the day, Papi brings him home.

Abuelo is tired and falls asleep for a while in his chair when he gets home. Mama covers him with a quilt.

Sometimes, when he wakes up, he looks upset and isn't sure where he is. But Mama talks to him in a soft voice until he feels better.

Then I take his hand and say, "Let's paint, Abuelo."
He looks down at me and smiles as we walk together to
the workbench.

I hand him his paintbrush. He nods and says, "Gracias, Chico."

Mama says, "Luis, Abuelo will have more and more trouble remembering things and recognizing people, maybe even you, but he will always be able to feel our love."

So I pick up my paintbrush and sit next to him. He smiles, and we paint together, Abuelo and me, his "Chico."

Dedicated to the memory of my abuelo,
my great-grandfather Pedro,
who enriched my childhood years
—DdA

To my Pop Pop, the epitome of gentleness and strength.
Every illustration in this book reminded me of our time together when
I was little. I love you, and I know you're watching over me.
—AH

Library of Congress Cataloging-in-Publication data is on file with the publisher.

Text copyright © 2019 by Diane de Anda
Illustrations copyright © 2019 by Alleanna Harris
First published in the United States of America in 2019 by Albert Whitman & Company
ISBN 978-0-8075-1492-4 (hardcover)
ISBN 978-0-8075-1493-1 (ebook)

All rights reserved. No part of this book may be reproduced or transmitted in any
form or by any means, electronic or mechanical, including photocopying,
recording, or by any information storage and retrieval system,
without permission in writing from the publisher.

Printed in China
10 9 8 7 6 5 4 3 2 1 HH 24 23 22 21 20 19

Design by Rick DeMonico

For more information about Albert Whitman & Company,
visit our website at www.albertwhitman.com.

100 Years of Albert Whitman & Company
Celebrate with us in 2019!

Picture DE ANDA

De Anda, Diane
The day Abuelo got
lost

10/02/19